First published 2016 by Nosy Crow Ltd
The Crow's Nest, 10a Lant Street
London SE1 1QR
www.nosycrow.com

ISBN 978 0 85763 982 0

Nosy Crow and associated logos are trademarks
and/or registered trademarks of Nosy Crow Ltd

John Lewis and associated logos are trademarks of John Lewis plc.
Text and illustrations © Nosy Crow Ltd 2016
Concept copyright © John Lewis plc 2016

The right of Sam Usher to be identified as the illustrator of this work has been asserted.

A CIP catalogue record for this book is available from the British Library.

Printed in Italy

Papers used by Nosy Crow are made from wood grown in sustainable forests.

1 3 5 7 9 8 6 4 2

Buster's Christmas

Written by Lucy Feather

Illustrated by Sam Usher

"It's nearly Christmas, Buster!"
Bridget said as it grew dark.
Buster raced towards the door
and gave a happy bark.

"It's bedtime now," said Mum to Bridget.
"Santa's on his way!
You'll have to stop your bouncing now.
It's time to sleep, not play."

Bridget really loved to bounce!
She gave one final leap,
then snuggled down into her bed
and soon was fast asleep.

Then outside in the garden, where the moon shone silver bright,
Dad crept across the frosty lawn – he'd work to do that night.
He tugged and tightened, hooked and tied,
then stopped and scratched his head.
He knew he had much more to do before he went to bed.

Until **at last** the job was done.
The net was in its place.
He turned and went into the house,
a smile upon his face.

While Bridget slept, the Christmas
lights were twinkling on the tree.
Mum and Dad sat side by side,
and snuggled cosily.

But as the clock struck midnight,
two young foxes sniffed the air.
They crept out of the shadows
and then stopped quite still to stare.

A thing was in the garden
that they'd never seen before.
A thing with nets and poles and steps –
they just had to explore!

The first bounce
was **surprising**,
and the second bounce
was **fun**.

The foxes jumped and
bounced with glee, until
they heard . . . someone.

That **someone** was a badger, who had seen their happy game.
She thought it looked **fantastic** and that she could do the same!

The same or even **better**,
because she was big and round.
She clambered up the ladder,
and she joined them with a **bound**.

Still on the sofa, Mum and Dad were cosy by the tree.
They didn't think to look outside and so they didn't see.
But Buster looked, and Buster saw! In this house, he was boss.
Those animals were on his patch. He felt a little cross!

But as he sat and watched them play, his eyes began to gleam.
He cocked his head and thought – he was a dog that had a dream…!

A squirrel and a hedgehog
joined the happy bouncing crew.
And Buster hatched a plan –
he knew exactly what to do!

The sun came up on Christmas Day, and Bridget woke up fast.
Had Santa filled her stocking and was Christmas here at last?
There were lots of little presents, more than she had ever seen . . .

But then she ran outside and saw . . .

. . . her brand-new trampoline!

Bridget jumped for joy –
this present was the very best.
She simply could not wait
to give that trampoline a test.

So off she ran, across the snow . . .

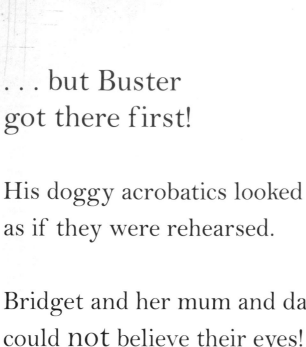

. . . but Buster
got there first!

His doggy acrobatics looked
as if they were rehearsed.

Bridget and her mum and dad
could not believe their eyes!
How had he learned
those clever tricks?
It was a big surprise!

It must be Christmas magic – an amazing bouncing spell!
But Buster kept his secret. He would never, ever tell . . .